A Girl Named Mister

Nikki Grimes

ZONDERVAN®

ZONDERVAN.com/
AUTHORTRACKER
follow your favorite authors

ZONDERVAN

A Girl Named Mister
Copyright © 2010 by Nikki Grimes

This title is also available as a Zondervan ebook.
Visit www.zondervan.com/ebooks.

This title is also available as a Zondervan audio edition.
Visit www.zondervan.fm.

Requests for information should be addressed to:
Zondervan, *Grand Rapids, Michigan* 49530

This edition: ISBN 978-0-310-72313-4 (softcover)

Library of Congress Cataloging-in-Publication Data

Grimes, Nikki.
    A girl named Mister / Nikki Grimes.
       p. cm.
       Summary: A pregnant teenager finds support and forgiveness from God through a
book of poetry presented from the Virgin Mary's perspective.
    ISBN 978-0-310-72078-2 (hardcover)
       [1. Novels in verse. 2. Pregnancy—Fiction. 3. Mary, Blessed Virgin, Saint—Fiction.
4. Christian life—Fiction. 5. African Americans—Fiction.] I. Title.
    PZ7.5.G75Gi 2010
    [Fic]—dc22

                  2010010830

Latin quotes are taken from *Latin Quips at Your Fingertips*, compiled and translated by Rose
Williams. Published by Barnes & Noble Books, 2001.

Cover design: DesignWorks
Cover photography: ©iStockphoto
Interior design & composition: Greg Johnson/Textbook Perfect & Carlos Eluterio Estrada

Printed in the United States of America

11 12 13 14 15 16 17 /DCI/ 23 22 21 20 19 18 17 16 15 14 13 12 11 10 9 8 7 6 5 4 3 2 1

A Girl
Named
Mister

013995198 0

Other books by Nikki Grimes:

Dark Sons

Voices of Christmas

Acknowledgements

This book had a long and circuitous journey, and many helped along the way.

First, the manuscript passed through the hands of editors Donna Bray, Arianne Lewin, and Jacque Alberta. I thank each for her part in helping to shape the story.

I owe a special debt of gratitude to Ginny M.M. Schneider and Gina Marie Mammano V. for reading early versions of the text. Your honest, intuitive response was a great encouragement.

Thanks, always, to my agent Elizabeth Harding, the best partner and cheerleader an author could have.

Finally, grateful thanks to Amy Wevodau Malskeit, who put in countless hours critiquing various drafts of this novel. Amy, words fail.

I hope I did you all proud.

Prologue

Mary: When Gabriel Comes

I.

A bright light turns the night
of my chamber into day
and pries my eyes open.
What do I see?
A being lit from within,
a giant whose voice
is quiet thunder.
"Fear not," he says, too late.
I quake, rubbing my eyes
anxious to wake
from this dream.
"I am Gabriel,"
says the voice, more soothing now.
"I bring a message from God."
Trembling, I rise
ready to listen.
Still, what am I to make
of his amazing words?
That I, a virgin,
am to be mother of Messiah?

II.

All things are possible
with God.
The truth of it
falls on me like rain.
I slowly drink it in,
then lift my arms,
surrendered.
"I am yours, Lord.
Do with me as you will."

He wraps his light
around me.

I am never the same again.

Mister: First Touch

How did it happen?
I told myself
it's only touching.
I told myself
my clothes are still on.
But who was I kidding?
Even through
my rayon-cotton blend
his touch
burned the world away.

Cave quicquam incipias quod paeniteat postea.

"Be careful about starting something you may regret."

— Syrus, *Maxims*

A Girl Named Mister

Blame it on my mother.
She's the one who named me
Mary Rudine.
The name is some throwback
her old-fashioned thinking
came up with.
Nobody but Mom
has called me Mary Rudine
since forever.
First it was Mary,
then it was M.R.
Mister is all anybody
calls me now.

My boyfriend used to think
it was cute,
a girl named Mister.
Used to think I was cute.
Used to be my boyfriend
what feels like
a million years ago.
Then again, I used to be
a good Christian girl,
the kind who would never, well ...
Just goes to show
how little people know.
Even I was surprised by me.
Now, I close my eyes
hoping to see
exactly where I went wrong.

When It Was Good

Was it that long ago?
I remember one morning
sitting in church,
keeping my eyes on Dante,
the cutest boy in the band.
Mom caught me.
"Quit eyeing that guitarist
like candy," she whispered.
I laughed easy.
In those days,
Mom and me,
we could talk
about anything.

Temple of My Redeemer

A second home,
as familiar as skin.
Crammed inside its walls
memories of
Sunday school,
all-church picnics,
and vacation Bible school
Sword drills.
My youth group meets there,
and choir, of course.
Even my old Girl Scout troop
once hung out
on holy ground,
meeting in
the church basement.
I could always
count on the deacons
to take dozens of cookies
off my hands.
I'm just saying,
God's house
was cozy territory,
no question.
Until this last year.
Don't ask me why,
but something in me
started pulling away.

Choir

For as long as I can remember,
I have loved to sing in the choir.
"Sing, Mister" folks call out
as my voice does a high-wire
reaching for heaven's hem.
I don't know what my friend Sethany
concentrates on,
but whenever she sings
about the Lord
her face gets this inside-out glow.
That's all I know.

Something's Missing

Ankle deep,
my faith a thing
I wade into now and then.
Not like Sethany.
She's mid-sea
and thinks I'm
right behind her.

For Me

I'm not sure when it happened,
but one Sunday I woke up
and for me,
church was mostly about
hanging out with friends
at God's house.
And for the longest time,
that seemed to be enough.
After worship,
Mom would flash me a smile
that said "Good girl!"
as Seth and I
trotted off
to youth group.

Restless

I turned the music
of the world
way up,
my feet itching to dance
to a new rhythm,
something other than
gospel.

Sophomore Shuffle

Mom calls volleyball
my new religion
just 'cause
I practice every day.
How else will I get better?
Let her razz me
all she wants.
I figure
since I was good enough
to make the team,
maybe volleyball
can help pay my way
to college.
It could happen.
You know what they say
about miracles.

Then Came Trey

It was a Tuesday.
It was almost cliché.
He raced round a corner,
rushing to class,
and smashed into me.
My books went flying
and so did my temper.
Thanks to this bonehead
I was going to be late,
which put me in no mood
for his apology,
and I was all ready
to cut him down to size
with my eyes,
until I caught his.
Those long lashes got me,
the way they softened
the hardscape of his face.
One look,
and they softened me too.
"Are you okay?" asked Trey.
I said something, I think,
or maybe I just nodded,
or smiled.
It's not my fault
I can't remember.
Blame it on
those stupid lashes.

Outsider

I asked around,
found out Trey
is one of those guys
who hangs out on the fringes
of our group.
He doesn't go to church
but seems to like
Christian kids,
so I figure
he probably believes in God.
That's one point
in his favor.

Just Friends

I never thought
he was perfect.
I won't tell myself
that lie.
But he was fine,
had a twinkle in his eye
with my name on it.
And when he smiled
I fell into him
headfirst,
got lost in his laughter.
I saw no danger.
After all,
we were just friends.

Trey's Girl

I remember the first time
he claimed me.
We were at a party
with a bunch of kids from school
just after Thanksgiving.
I'd gone with Sethany.
Trey had shown up on his own,
like always.
Seth and I were chatting away
when some guy
from a school 'cross town
came up to me for a dance.
Before I had a chance to speak,
Trey threw me a look,
then got all in this guy's face,
smiling though
and saying nice as anything,
"Excuse me, but
this is my girl."

Dylan Thomas

Trey found me in the library,
surprised me with a kiss
on the back of my neck.
The heat of it
ran up and down my spine
and I'm thinking,
Dylan who?
"See you later," Trey whispers.
distracting me a little more
for good measure.
So, of course,
I had to go back
to the top of the page
and start reading
"Do Not Go Gentle
Into that Good Night"
all over again.

Into Him

I can't usually stand know-it-all
b-ball players,
but I liked the way
Trey committed to
steering clear of drugs,
and how he talked about
keeping his body pure —
something we had in common,
even though I know
it doesn't mean the same
for him and me.
Maybe, one day
it will.

Date

Trey said he'd be happy
to hang out with me wherever,
so I invite him to video night
at church.
Soon as the lights wink out
in the rec room
and *Princess Bride*
blinks onto the screen
(never mind that we've all seen
it a gazillion times!),
Trey whispers in my ear
that he wants me all to himself.
No more of these group dates
on video night,
or lame trips (his words)
to the local skating rink
for spins around the ice
and cups of hot chocolate.
"Why can't we,
you know,
go on a real date,
just you and me?"
Yeah, why not?
I start thinking.
Why not?

Don't Remind Me

"Careful," Seth warned me.
"I see the way you look at Trey,
the way he looks at you.
Remember, we both promised God
we'd wait."
"We're not doing anything," I told her.
We're not doing anything,
I told myself.
Still, I couldn't help but notice
how the purity band
on my ring finger
seemed loose lately.
Like any day now,
it might
just
slip
off.

Just Us

Alone at his house,
his parents I don't know where,
we sit on the sofa,
the TV watching the heat
rising between us.
I tingle all over
as Trey closes the distance.
It's okay,
I tell myself.
I won't let it go
too far.
But before I know it,
his hand is rubbing my inner thigh,
racing toward my waist,
reaching underneath my—
What am I doing?
"Stop!" I tell him
using what little breath
I have left,
too trapped
in my own frustration
to worry
about his.

Exposure

I switch on the TV,
see this boy and girl
plastered against the wall
of some fictional school,
kissing their brains out,
then sneaking inside the boys' room.
Together.
I shudder, slightly disgusted,
and turn away.
Still, I start to wonder
if all the other
kids are right.
Am I Miss Priss?
Am I making too big a deal
about waiting?

The "L" Word

"You're so beautiful," says Trey,
his hands busy
with my buttons.
I finger the cross
round my neck.
A voice inside me chides
Remember:
You're saving yourself for true love.
Trey must've heard.
How else to explain
him suddenly
cupping my face in his hands
and whispering,
"You're killing me, girl.
You know I'm falling
in love with you."

MTV

Nelly's "Body on Me"
filters through the window.
I close my eyes,
wait for the music to end,
but I still can't sleep.
The beat of my thoughts
a rhythm I can't get
out of my head.
I just want you.
I just want to be
your addiction—
lines from a song
stirring in me
and the CD
isn't even on.

Losing Ground

Like a summer shower
falling in silver sheets
thick as curtains,
love rains down on me.
Love
and love
and love
and Trey
are all I see.

In the Name of Love

I can't explain it.
I think *Trey*
and feel as if
I've swallowed warm honey
and a spoonful of sun.
I'm not that pretty,
still I'm the one
he wants.
Don't ask me why.
I only know
it makes me happy.
And isn't that what love is?
And isn't love what God is?
So how can wanting more of this
be wrong?

Amnesia

Trey strokes my bare shoulder
and I shudder as
once-familiar words burst
like fireworks in my brain.
Something Pastor said about
temptation, and God's help.
What was it?
I start to push away,
to study the words before
they fade.
"You're sweet as
a chocolate Sunday,"
whispers Trey.
I smile, close my eyes,
and wait for more.
Before I know it,
my eyelids are screens
flashing the words
Your body is a temple
of the—
"Silk wishes it were
as soft as you,"
Trey interrupts,
blowing hotly in my ear.
And after that, I swear
I don't remember
much of anything.

Trey's Place

Oh, God, oh, God! His hands
mapping every inch of me,
journeying where they shouldn't be
but, ooooh!
Lord, I know you'll understand.
You made my skin, Trey's hand.
I never knew it could feel so—
What's he doing?
Mmmm. He's tracing my name
across my belly,
Mister, each letter
wet from his tongue.
God, I'm sorry but
I can't stop,
don't want to—
Oh God, oh God, Oh
God will forgive me,
right?
Right?

Later

He sleeps, guiltless.
I slink out of bed,
slither into wrinkled shirt and jeans,
pretend I'm a shadow
creeping across the floor,
slipping out the door,
racing home quick as feet
can meet the air.
But no matter how fast I flee,
step by step
guilt gains on me.

Thoughts on the Long Walk Home

I.
It's not that I thought
angels would sing,
or the sky would part.
I'm not a kid.
But I did think
there'd be this trade,
that I'd give something up
and he would too.
Instead,
I'm somehow less
and his more
is still locked away
in a mystery
of bone and skin,
and the sin of it
is that I'm empty now,
and keyless.

II.
It wasn't worth
all the guilt,
I know that much.
Besides, once he got past
the feeling-up part,
it was mostly pain.
Why do all those
stupid songs say
the first time
is the best?

III.
What would Seth say?
I'm not ready to tell her, yet.
Not ready to see the look in her eye,
the one that says
What happened to the promise
you made to God?

Sorry

I wish it was easier
breaking God's law.
I wish that commitment band
didn't burn my finger
like lye.
I snatched it off that night,
opened my bedroom window
and tossed it.
If Mom asks where it's gone,
I'll say I lost it.
What's one more lie?
I already told God
I didn't mean it,
that I hadn't planned
to give myself away.
But just between me and you,
that's only half true.

Thought Soup

My mind's a mess.
Wasn't it yesterday
I looked for Trey around
every corner, down every hall?
Now, for the last three days
all I do
is duck whenever
he comes into view.
I need time to think,
to figure out
what I'm feeling
and why.

Instant Message

I switch on the computer
Mom worked overtime
to pay for,
check my IM
and click on slickwillow,
the screenname Coach
gave my best friend, Sethany,
'cause she's tall and willowy,
and the enemy always
counts her out,
thinking she's a girly-girl.
But once she hits the court,
look out,
'cause she's a slammer,
and God help the girl
across from Sethany
when she's at the net.
"hey! waz up?"
The words pop
on the computer screen.
"before you answer,
wat's a 6 letter wd
for sequester?"
"wat's sequester?" I write.
"sigh. that's y U cant
beat me at Scrabble.
U have heard of the dictionary?"
"whatever," I write.
"i've got more important things
on my mind."
"oooh! this is going 2 be hot,
i can tell." ☺

"well, i was with Trey last week."

"and?"

"i — was — with — Trey last week."

"OMG," Sethany writes. (:0)

"exactly."

Wish

I didn't tell Seth this,
but I wish I had waited.
I know, God.
You wish I had too.
How come your voice
is coming through loud and clear now?
Why couldn't I hear you before?
Never mind. I know.
Call me Jonah.
I was too busy running
in the opposite direction.
Just one more thing
for which I have to take the blame.

New Territory

The next day
Seth nods to me
across the classroom,
like always.
Except there's something off
about her silent hello,
a look that says
I guess I don't know you
as well as I thought.

Email

"Waz up, girl?
Hardly seen u since —
u know.
I'm missing u.
When can we meet?
Trey."
I hit delete.
Wish I could do the same
with that one, wrong night.

Let's Talk

The next day
Trey meets me after class.
He leans in for a kiss.
I love those lips
and get lost in them, for a minute.
But then I come to my senses.
"Trey, we need to talk."
He pulls back.
"What's wrong?"
"Nothing. I mean—"
My hands go clammy.
"I don't want to talk here."
"Let's go to my place then."
A siren goes off in my head.
His place? Alone? Again?
"Fine," I tell us both,
promising myself
this time will be different.

Dr. Jekyll

Inside the door,
Trey drops our backpacks
on the floor,
and reaches for me
as if he's grown
an extra pair of hands.
They're everywhere —
at my buttons,
fiddling with my zipper.
I push him away.
"Stop it, Trey.
We can't do this.
I can't do this.
I'm sorry."
Trey goes stone-still,
then drops his hands
to his sides.
His eyes go glacial.
"I'm sorry," I repeat.
"Whatever.
I need to hit the shower.
You know where the door is."
"But Trey —"
"Go run hot and cold
somewhere else."

Do-Over

It's me.
I must've done
something wrong,
not made myself clear.
I mean, he loves me, right?
So it shouldn't matter
if we're not together
like that.
Maybe if I just
explain it to him right.
I'll try again, tonight.

Phone Call

He won't return
my texts, or phone calls.
It's all I can do
not to wait for him
at the gym
after basketball practice.
I just want to ask
what happened to him loving me?
Why can't we still be
together?
I don't understand.
He said I was his girl.
He said he was my man.

Vanishing Act

Days disappear in a haze
of Shakespeare, career fairs,
pop quizzes, history homework,
and the white noise of teachers
calling on me
for answers I've suddenly forgotten
how to give.

Reality Check

I'm slow.
But even I know
this isn't going to work.
Just try telling that
to my heart.

Exit

My head keeps spinning.
I need some space to think.
Later that day, I say to Trey,
"Look. I can see
you want to cool it for a while,
so let's."
Trey is all shrugs.
I wonder what that means,
but not for long.
"Yeah, well," says Trey.
"Whatever."
I suddenly shiver
in the winter
of his words.

Pit Stop

The bathroom
seems light-years away.
I barely make it
before the flood of tears
puts my shame on display.
It's official.
I live in regret.
That's the black room
at the end of the hall.
Call before you come.
I may not be
in the mood for company.

The Book

These days, I wake
and look at The Book,
a familiar stranger
collecting dust
on my bedside table.
I haven't felt the weight of it
in my hands for weeks.
How can I even
call it mine anymore?
I know the score.
It's fragile pages
make it clear:
sex outside of marriage is sin.
Spin it any way you like,
I blew it.
One voice tells me
to search the Psalms
for forgiveness.
Another says
Don't go crying to God now.
And so I pull away and stew
in a new kind of loneliness.

Substitute

I slip into my mother's room,
raid the small shelf by her bed
hunting for a book a little less holy,
some story about God twice removed.
I know its crazy,
but I need to feel Him here,
just not too near,
you know?
There was this one book I remember,
something Mom used to bug me to read.
What was it?
I scratch my memory
with a finger of thought.
Come on, Mister. Think!
I tell myself.
But it's no use.
Frustrated, I take it out
on her door,
slamming it on my way out.
Good thing Mom wasn't
home from work,
or I'd never hear
the end of it.

In Plain Sight

I collapse into Mom's recliner
and reach for the remote,
my drug of choice.
My fingers graze the cover
of a dog-eared book
sitting face-up on the end table.
The title clicks:
Mary, Mary.
That's it!
The book of poetry my mom
has loved forever,
a book about Christ's mother.
I quickly scan
the first few pages,
find the language
a little old-timey.
Still, it reads like a diary,
and the mystery of that
makes it worth
trading in the remote.
I slip the slim volume
into my jeans pocket
for the short ride to my room.
I figure I'll flip through
a few pages before
hitting the homework
like I'm supposed to.
That's the plan.

Stirring Memory

Our golden boy
nestles in my arms,
clutching my breast
nursing, oblivious
to the braying of donkeys,
the mooing of cows,
and the smell of offal
pervading this stable
in the heart of Bethlehem.
Joseph hangs over my shoulder,
his face a mask of wonderment.
I sigh, no less in awe
than he.
Husband.
Mother.
Son.
These new words
roll round my mind
like shiny marbles,
bursting with color and light.
Was it truly only
nine months ago
I blushed
at the very idea of a wedding bed?
So much has happened since then.
I close my eyes, straining to remember
a time before the angel Gabriel,
a time before the Lord Jehovah
visited just long enough
to turn my world
upside down.

Silent Conversation

Early evening
is my favorite time of day.
I take my time
winding down the hills of Nazareth
to the village well.
My feet know the way
so I can concentrate on enjoying
my silent conversation
with Jehovah:
me meditating on his word,
Him speaking to my heart.
Some evenings,
when the wind strokes my cheek,
I can almost hear him
call my name.

Dawn

Playful pouting is not seemly,
Father told me,
not during the holiest of seasons,
and perhaps he was right.
But I do not understand
why I must be
as heavy and somber as he
at Passover.
The coming festival fills me
with joy —
a few days away from Nazareth,
another chance to stand
in the temple of our God,
another opportunity
to feel the sway
of sweet psalms sung
by the Levite choir there.
Why should such wonders
weigh me down with the sadness
I see on Father's face?
Mother reminds me
that each of us comes to Passover
with a different heart.
What matters, she tells me,
is that we give that heart
to God.
Her wisdom is enough
to send me to Father's side.
"Forgive me, Father," I say.
"Let me help you pack
for the journey."

A Thing to Ponder

I lie on my pallet that night
wondering what it was like
when the Angel of Death
stole the firstborn
of all under Egypt's wing,
save those blessed ones
whose homes were blood-marked
for salvation,
those faithful Jews
who knew God was
as good as his word:
Pharaoh's kingdom would suffer
until he set God's people free.
Would I have shuddered
as the Shadow of Death
passed me by?
Would I have had
enough breath left
to praise Jehovah?
And now, because of that
long-ago night,
we Jews are free,
Pharaoh having lost
his taste for Jewish slaves,
the life of his young son
a price too high
after all.

Jerusalem, City of God

The latter rains
have wet the earth,
but my poor eyes
are dry as the desert wind.
The three-day journey to Jerusalem
punishes with aching calves
and blistered feet.
Why is it I always manage to forget
the tedium of this trek?
I feel a complaint
rising to my lips,
but bite it back
when I remember holy Scripture.
"Let the Israelites keep the Passover
at the appointed time."
I chew on God's words,
determining to put one foot
in front of the other.
I shade my eyes
and look ahead,
finding my betrothed in the distance,
his gait as steady as it was
when we left Nazareth.
He may be closer to my father's age than mine,
but Joseph will make a fine husband,
I think for the hundredth time.
Then I'm distracted
by the glittering jewel
rising out of the desert:
Jerusalem!
The setting sun bounces golden
off the walls of the temple

where Jehovah resides,
and my heart beats faster.
I awake to new strength
surging through me,
and lengthen my stride.
As we draw closer to the Holy City,
I pick up the pace,
pausing every now and then
to wipe away my tears.

Reflection

Back home in Nazareth,
my family and I
relax after dining,
sated with food and new memories
of the Passover festival.
The songs of the Levite choir
still ring in my ears.
My soul carried them with me
like waterskins,
refreshment for
the long journey home.
The glint in my father's eye
reminds me of
the golden incense holder
I've heard men speak of.
I have never glimpsed it
from the Court of Women.
Pity that we're not permitted
to see the holy sacrifices
for ourselves.
Though, truth be told,
I would rather not watch
an animal have its throat slit.
Still.
"You know, Father," I say.
"Next year at the Passover,
I believe I'll enter the Court of Israel
to witness the sacrifices firsthand."
Father almost drops his cup of wine.
"What?"
"They say a woman did so once before.
Besides, am I not as much

a child of God as any man?"
Father's eyes flash toward Mother.
"Speak to your daughter!"
Mother gives me her sternest look,
for Father's benefit,
then, when he turns away,
we share a secret smile.
Later, as we clean the cooking pots,
she tells me,
"I see what joy it gives you
to frighten your father.
But I ask you,
why settle for being equal with men?"
My mother's bold words
make me love her more,
and I pledge myself to walk
in her strength.
Someday, I hope my children
will walk in mine.

Gabriel

Familiar as my bedchamber is,
I miss the temple.
Not the raucous crowds,
or the squeal of lambs
or squawk of pigeons
readied for the sacrifice,
but His Presence.
I met God in the temple,
and he knew me.
In some strange way,
I even feel him here.
I snuggle down
on my sleeping mat,
and close my eyes.
But not for long.
An angel slips into my room,
announces that God is on his way,
then tells me I am to be mother
of Messiah, the Promised One,
the Savior of our people;
that my once-barren cousin Elizabeth,
too old to bear a child,
bears one now.
What sense am I
to make of that?
I rub my eyes,
waiting to wake,
unable to shake this vision.

Mary: Light Show

Lord?
What is happening?
I feel a gentle warmth
settling over me,
fingers of heat
fluttering from naval to knee.
Am I dreaming?
What is this cloud of light?
I close my eyes
and count to three,
but when I look again,
the shadow without darkness
is still swallowing me whole.
I poke its side,
then hide my face
when my touch
sends up sparks without flame.
Lord,
what is this cool fire
that licks my skin,
and why do I tingle so?
Gabriel?
Is this what you meant?
Gabriel?
Are you still there?

The Morning After

Who will believe me?
Who?
And what if no one does?
What then?
I march through the next day
numb, that one question
circling my mind
like a vulture
ready to pick my thoughts clean.
I feel my belly,
flat as ever,
and close my eyes,
remembering the fire
of God's touch,
hearing the echo of the word
Messiah.

Betrothed

And what about Joseph?
We are as good as married,
our betrothal
as binding as any other,
and nothing less than
a paper of divorcement
could end it.
Of course, we have never
shared a bed,
nor will we
until our wedding night.
So, if I truly am with child,
Joseph will know
the father
is someone else.
And what will Joseph —
No. I am not yet ready
to consider
what hard or bitter things
might await me
in the distance.
Besides, the Lord Jehovah
will meet me there.
Yes?

Interruption

"Are you deaf?"
My mother's voice penetrates,
unwelcome,
reaching me easily from downstairs.
"What?"
"Is your homework done?"
she asks.
I trade *Mary, Mary* for my notebook,
and yell down "Soon!"
That's as close to the truth
as I can manage.
Lucky for me, I'm a good student.
By the time she calls "Lights out,"
I'm done.
I flip the switch.
"Goodnight," says Mom.
"Goodnight," I answer.
I place *Mary, Mary* beneath my pillow
and feel a little closer
to God.

Clarity

Where have I been?
I wake and look around
as if the world is new,
or old.
I can't tell which,
only that
the fog inside my head
is lifted
and I can think again.
I can see.

Trey was bad for me.
Time to move on.

Focus

Off to school.
English lit to study.
Friends to concentrate on.
Volleyball to play.
Pray coach and teachers
don't call on you.
Got lots of catching up to do.

Split

Long as I can remember,
Seth and me,
we were two peas
in a pod,
exactly alike
in every way.
That's no longer true
and there's nothing I can do
to change things back.
We're in different places now,
like I entered a room
Seth doesn't have a key to
and the best we can do
is wave through the window.
I just hope one day soon
I'll figure out how
to crack that window open
an inch or two,
without, you know,
smashing it to bits.

A Simple Question

Somewhere between
bites of pepperoni
and a swig of milk,
Seth asks,
"So, what's with you and Trey?
Are you, you know,
hooking up now?"
I almost choke,
no joke.
Milk sputters
down my chin.
I grab a napkin,
start dabbing away,
my brain on fire
from the fuse
she just lit.
"It was one time, Seth!"
I say, teeth tight.
"One time!
And I'm already sorry."
"Okay, okay!" says Seth.
"I was—you know—
just wondering."
I cut my eyes at her.
"Okay!" she says.
"I'll shut up."
That is
the smartest thing
she's said
all day.

Choir Practice

All through practice,
Seth snatches looks at me,
as if she's wondering
what I'm doing here.
I want to yell,
"Virgins aren't the only ones
who can sing!"
But who am I kidding?
I *do* feel weird being here,
singing about a God
I broke my promise to.
If everybody knew,
maybe they'd ask me to leave,
and maybe I would.
And maybe I should.

Private Matters

"Haven't seen Sethany
around here much lately,"
says my mom.
"You two get in a fight?"
"No," I say. "We're both busy, is all."
I study the wall
just right of her head,
hoping she doesn't notice
how adept I'm getting
at avoiding eye contact,
wishing she wasn't
so dang nosey.

A Crack in the Window

"We broke up, by the way,"
I told Seth over lunch.
She quit munching her sandwich
long enough to look up
to see if I was okay.
I didn't say anything,
just shrugged my shoulders
in a way that said *Don't ask.*
Not now.
She took the cue,
smiled to let me know
she was relieved,
and finished eating
in silence.

Face-to-Face

I miss the old days
before I pulled away from church,
when I trusted Seth
with all my secrets,
even face-to-face.
Funny how my fears
weighed half as much back then,
as if telling my best friend
split them in two.
I used to say or do whatever
and never worry
that she'd judge me
or love me less.
If only we could be
that close again.
What if I took a chance
and let her in?

Truth Time

"Here's the ugly truth,"
I tell Seth after school.
"Trey never really
cared for me.
He just wanted
to add me to his list."
I ball my fist,
fighting back the tears.
Seth slips an arm around me.
"It'll be alright," she chokes out.
"Besides," she adds,
"he's not worth the dirt
under your fingernails.
He's a supercilious, joyless jerk."
Clearly, Seth's been
hitting the dictionary again,
which makes me smile
in the middle of my cry,
which is exactly why
I love her.

Back to Normal

Later that week,
I finish up an essay for English
as my cell phone rings,
putting a period on my homework
for the night.
It's Seth, of course,
calling to remind me
about Youth Group Video Night.
"It'll probably be lame," she says.
"Ya think? Bet you anything
it'll be *The Princess Bride*."
"Again!" we say in unison.
"Come hang with me anyway,"
pleads Sethany.
"We always have a blast."
*"Escuchame, pero
yo no hablo Ingles,"* I say.
"Girl! Quit it!"
We ping-pong words
back and forth awhile
before I finally say yes.
I can't help but smile
at the ease of it,
feeling like we're almost
back to normal.

Switch

His heart must be
a light switch,
something he turns on and off
whenever the mood hits,
'cause here he is,
weeks later,
pressing another girl
up against the hall lockers.
I can't fly by
fast enough.
What was that line again?
"You're killing me, girl.
You know I'm falling
in love with you."
Yeah.
Right.
Color me stupid.

I Want to be Alone

The school library
is suddenly my best friend.
I sneak there
for a quick rendezvous
with *Mary*.

Dinner

Joseph joins my family
for the evening meal,
the first we have shared
since it happened.
Does it show?
Does my face glow
like the skin of Moses
on Mt. Sinai?
"Shalom, Joseph," I greet him,
quickly dropping my gaze,
afraid my secret is sealed
in the glint of my eye.
"How was your day?"
"The trek to Sepphoris was grueling
in this midsummer heat,
especially the climb
up that last, steep hill.
But you know, Sepphoris is
our nearest metropolis,
and that is where the work is.
So, I go." I nod to show
that I am listening,
all the while wondering
why Mother didn't hear us,
why a man,
righteous as my father,
couldn't sense
the presence of God
in his own house.
Unless God did not want him to.
"I worked on cabinets today,"
says Joseph.

"Or should I say
they worked on me.
My muscles scream.
Surely, you must hear them."
"Poor Joseph," I tease.
"Maybe I can help."
Rising from the table,
I plant my strong young hands
onto his stiff old shoulders
and knead the pain away.
"You are an angel," says Joseph.
I smile to myself, thinking
No. But last night,
I met one.

Haunted

When Mother greeted me
this morning,
my only answer was a nod.
I refuse to speak until sundown,
this one-day vow of silence
the least I can do
to help me focus,
sort truth from wild imagination.
After all, where is the evidence
that my visit from
Gabriel and God
was more than a dream?
The very idea seems
impossible to me now,
that somehow Jehovah
would place
his son in *me*.
Three days have passed,
and life remains common
as birdsong and morning
as I move swiftly through
the market at Sepphoris,
careful to guard my purse
from the sly fingers
of small thieves.
I am here to purchase
fresh coriander and thyme,
but a tumbling mound of
luscious pomegranates
tipping the scales
of a nearby merchant
tempts me to add a few

to my basket.
I reach for one,
only to drop it when I hear
"Gabriel?"
My heart races at the sound.
"Gabriel?"
I spin round to discover
the source of my distraction.
It is a young woman,
not much older than me.
Could it really be?
Does she see the angel too?
I rush toward her,
my mind fumbling for
words to ask that
impossible question.
Two steps away,
my lips part just as
a little boy darts
from behind a market stall.
"Gabriel," she scolds, "how often
must I tell you not to run from me
in the marketplace?"
I lower my head and turn away,
feeling foolish.
And yet, I cannot shake the feeling
of that holy presence
in my bedchamber,
nor any longer deny
that the archangel's voice
still rings in my ear.
Did he not say
he knew of my cousin, Elizabeth?
That Jehovah had visited her too?

Once and for all,
I must learn if it is true.
I head home to pack.
My puny purchases
can wait.
I must journey to Judah.
I must speak with Elizabeth.

Journey to Judah

Lamech, a servant of Joseph,
joins me, huddling beneath
an acacia tree.
The sun threatens to peel me
like a grape,
and I am grateful for
this circle of shade,
though I would hate
for these deadly thorns
to pierce my skin.
I slide to the ground,
and lean against the trunk,
tensing at the sound
of a lion's roar
in the distance.
Thankfully,
judging from the direction
of the sound, we are downwind
of his scent.
"Here," says Lamech,
offering his waterskin
before slaking his own thirst.
I smile at his kindness,
remembering the Bedouin proverb
my father never tired of repeating:
Always take care
of the stranger,
for one day,
you may be the stranger.
"Learn this wisdom,"
my father said,

"for no one survives alone
in the wilderness."
"Drink deep," says Lamech.
"Only a camel travels miles
on a single sip."
I reach for the waterskin,
and drink my fill.
"Come, Lamech," I say,
springing to my feet.
"We must not allow this heat
to slacken our pace.
The hills of Judah call to me,
and I wish to see my cousin's face
by nightfall."

Sharing Secrets

Zechariah meets us at the gate,
smiling wordlessly.
I assume, as priest,
he has taken a vow of silence,
and think no more of it.
He leads us to the inner court.
Elizabeth welcomes us
with cups of pomegranate juice,
as Lamech and I having been
spotted some distance away.
"Shalom!" Elizabeth calls to us.
As I draw near,
I rehearse what I will say,
what I will ask:
Cousin, what do you know
of angels? Of Gabriel himself?
I have to know!
But, before teeth touch tongue
and my words begin to flow,
Elizabeth declares,
"Blessed are you among women,
and blessed is the fruit of your womb!"
God's spirit descends on me
like mist, and through my tears
I notice the swell
of Elizabeth's belly.
Six months with child,
Gabriel had said,
and so it seems.
I drop my cup
and lift my hands to heaven.
"My soul does magnify
the Lord!"

Evidence

Elizabeth has a word for this
disease churning my stomach
like rancid butter,
for the way my nostrils swell
at the very smell
of warm goat's milk,
for this faint feeling of floating
miles from lake or ocean swell.
It is a feeling Cousin
has come to know well,
and she calls it
Proof.

Shrinkwrap

I noticed this morning
the snap on my favorite jeans
seemed to have changed zip codes.
I could hardly hitch the zipper
into place. Shoot.
Mom better give
that new detergent
the boot.

Hands Off

Late for volleyball drills,
I race to the locker room,
dump my open backpack
on the bench, and strip
faster than Clark Kent.
I climb into my gym clothes,
moving too fast to catch Seth
flipping through my copy
of *Mary, Mary.*
"What's this?" she asks.
I look up, snatch the book,
and stuff it back into my pack,
totally ignoring the *O* of Seth's mouth.
"Well, excuse me!" she says,
meaning nothing of the kind.
But I don't care.
Some things you just don't share.
Mary, Mary is mine alone.
At least for now.

Close

Funny how a person in a book
can come to life.
It's like I know Mary now,
like we've been kicking it
half of forever.
I never thought about her
being funny, or tough,
or brave enough to travel
through the wilderness
where there were lions,
just so she could see her cousin.
All I have to do to see mine
is hop the subway.
No way I would have made it
back then.
But I'm glad Mary
can take me along
for the ride.

Guidance Counselor

Miss Wells,
the guidance counselor,
flips through papers on her desk.
I sit across from her,
breathing heavy,
tapping my no-name sneakers
on the floor,
waiting for her to get started,
so she can finish,
so I can go.
"You kids just can't
sit still, can you?"
I know a rhetorical question
when I hear one.
"So, Mister—
that's what they call you,
right?
What are your plans
after graduation?"
"To go to college," I answer,
without missing a beat.
"To major in what?"
She's got me there.
"You should start
thinking about that," she says.
"More importantly,
think about ways
to beef up your transcripts.
Find more extracurricular activities
that will look good on paper."
Yeah, I'm thinking.
That's what I need,
'cause I'm not busy enough already.

She's Right, Though

You didn't hear that
from me.
But I should get serious
about college.
Let's face it,
I'm gonna need
all the scholarships
I can get.
Nix on the glee club.
I've already got choir.
Can't stand politics,
so class council is out.
Hmmm.
For the rest of the day,
as I pass from class to class,
I scan the hall bulletin boards,
half hoping for ideas.
One ad jumps out:
a call for tutors
in the library literacy program.
Ding, ding, ding!
If there's one thing
I love to do, it's read.
That ad
might as well have
screamed out my name.

Rehearsal

It's eight weeks since Trey,
and I am almost over him.
In two days,
it'll be our choir's turn
to rock the house,
and four-part harmony
never sounded so good.
I close my eyes,
let my soprano raise the roof,
and before I know it
I'm lost in the music,
rubbing shoulders with God,
my faith as natural and easy
as it used to be.
I can't explain how,
but Mary must be getting to me.

Queasy

My stomach sloshes like
I'm at sea.
What's the matter with me?
Is this some new version of PMS?
Guess it could be.
It's been awhile
since my last period.
But that's one good thing
about being a girl jock.
I don't get periods
as often as other girls.
The sight of eggs
sunny-side up
makes me want to hurl.
"Honey, what's wrong?"
asks Mom, shuffling into the kitchen
in Sunday slippers.
"You look a little pale.
I hate for you to miss church,
but you can stay home
if you're feeling ill."
"Thanks, Mom," I say,
halfway to the bathroom.
"I think I will."

Twinge

My eyes follow Trey
down the central stairway.
"Snap out of it," says Seth,
watching me.
I know she's right,
but I still feel a twinge
when Trey slips his arm
over some other girl's shoulders.
Good thing I ended it.
Imagine how much worse I'd feel
if we had gotten serious,
and he had dumped me
for the next cute girl
to come along?
And what if I'd gotten pregnant,
or caught some nasty disease?
Like Seth said,
I don't even know
where his thing has been.
I shake my head
and leave all thoughts of Trey,
and possible disasters, behind.
I know I was lucky this time.

Locker Room

We're pulling on
our uniforms,
Sethany next to me,
both of us getting ready
for the big game against
Cleveland High.
"You're getting quite
a pooch there," Sethany says.
"Time you lay off those
potato chips."
She was just being flip,
but I cringe,
having to admit
my waistline seems to be
wandering a bit.
Better hit that floor
and work those drills double time.
That oughta shake off
a pound or two.

Fifteenth Birthday

A sleepover
is all I asked for.
Nothing fancy since
I know we can't afford it.
Mom makes a fuss anyway,
takes me and Seth out for dinner,
bakes my favorite carrot cake
with cream cheese icing,
and serves it with a tiny jewelry box.
Inside, I find a promise ring,
just like the one I tossed,
the one I'd said I lost.
"I know how much
it means to you," Mom says,
and I cry, because my lie
has made us less close
than we used to be.
"It's okay, baby," she says.
"Sorry," I whisper,
wiping my wet cheek.
Meanwhile, Sethany studies
her perfect nail polish,
keeping her knowledge to herself.
"Now blow out your candles!" Mom says,
giving my shoulder a squeeze.
"And don't forget to make a wish."
I'd tell her I'm too old for this,
but I know what she'd say:
Nobody's too old for wishing.

Squint

Saturday, I stroll Broadway
hunting mangos for Mom.
I slow in front of
Fashion Passion,
and drool over cool clothes
hanging in the window.
A girl with a too-thick waist
stares back at me
and I wonder why she's
wasting time
checking out
these clingy numbers.
Do I know her?
I step closer to the window,
squint, spy the mirror
behind the mannequins,
and — Oh!
Guess it's time
for me to go
on a diet.

Sea Sick

LaVonne Taylor waddles into
the cafeteria today,
four months along but looking six.
Kids laugh as she passes by,
but I don't see
what's so funny.
In fact, I think
it's pretty sad.
She's still a kid,
only fifteen years old,
same age as—
Something nasty rises in me,
like a flood:
thoughts of my pancake breasts
suddenly swelling like dough;
a growing list of shirts and jeans
too shrunken to fit;
waistline slowly vanishing
like some magic act gone wrong;
and way too many bloodless days
on the calendar.
I feel myself
start to drown,
make a gurgling sound,
and, next thing I know,
the school nurse
is leaning over me,
asking, "Honey, are you okay?"
"No. God, no!" I say,
but not to her.
How long I laid on her
office cot, crying,

I'll never know.
But at some point,
a soothing voice
deep in the core of me
whispered, *"Breathe. Breathe."*
And I did.

Prayer

I clutch *Mary, Mary*
to my chest,
waiting for sanity
to return.
"Help me, Mary,"
I whisper.
"Help me, God."

Kinswoman

Elizabeth and I
sit in the synagogue
where women are assigned,
rapt in twin silences,
but separate thoughts.
Elizabeth beams,
clearly more than ready
to slip into a mother's sandals.
But I shiver, wondering
what kind of mother
I will be.
I know so little of babies.
Will caring for a child
come naturally?
I can only hope to match
my own mother.
But where do I begin?
Then, I remember the story:
how Mother wrestled
with the Lord, in prayer,
pleading for a child,
and how, when I came,
she blessed God for the gift.
So, I will start with prayer.
Jehovah, please prepare me
to be a mother.
And Jehovah, I pray
as you knit this child
inside of me,
strengthen him
in every way.

Names

We sit in the evening glow
of oil lamps,
plucking names from the night
like figs,
as if we needed to.
But why not?
This is precisely what
expectant mothers do.
So, for a moment,
we pretend God has not
already chosen our sons' names.
"Eli has a nice sound," I say.
"Or Ezekiel," says Elizabeth.
"I like Tobias."
"Too plain."
"Uriah?"
"Never!"
"You are right.
Things did not
turn out well for him."
"Here is one, then: David,"
says Elizabeth.
"Like the king," I say.
"Like your ancestor."
"The one through whom —"
"Messiah will come," we both say,
and something in me quivers.
I excuse myself for the night,
needing to lose myself for a while
in the world of sleep.

Good-bye

I hug my quiet kinsman,
Zechariah,
and wish Elizabeth well,
though I hardly need to.
The blessed birth of her son
is only a few
weeks away at most,
and she is blissful.
I leave her in the able care
of her midwife,
and say my last good-byes.
Lord Jehovah,
make the months fly
until we are together again,
until her little John
meets my Jesus.

Neighborly

Entering Nazareth, once again
we come upon a riotous crowd,
closed tight around
someone, or thing.
We cannot tell
till Nathan, our neighbor, yells,
"Harlot!
You thought you could
break God's law, and live?"
We next hear
stone striking bone.
A girl screams and I,
unblinking,
push into the crowd,
elbowing my way up front
just as limestone brick
splits the girl's skull,
sending blood rushing
like a wild river,
flooding her eyes, her nose,
splattering her once
rosy cheeks.
I peek, now,
from half-closed lids,
wondering what holds me here,
why I continue to stare
at this poor, crumpled girl,
writhing in pain until death
rescues her, a girl I knew
as Salome, young wife of Hillel,
a girl who so easily
could be—

"Mary!" Joseph's servant
reaches my side.
"Let us leave this place," he says
and I let him pull me away.
Wordlessly, we head home.
But I carry this girl's
wretched screams with me,
like a splinter throbbing
in my ear.

Poison

I begged the nurse
not to call my mom,
said I probably just had
food poisoning, or something,
and apologized for crying
like a big baby.
The nurse shook her head,
put the phone down,
looked me in the eye, and said,
"Mary Rudine, my guess is
you're less than
three months along.
Take my advice:
Tell your mother before
she figures it out
on her own.
You shouldn't try
handling this alone."
I dropped my eyes,
grabbed my books,
and ran.

Team Spirit

Coach says
I have none
since I'm leaving the team
at the end of the season,
just before the biggest game.
"You looking to play
in the city club off-season?
'Cause I gotta tell ya,
this ain't the way
to hold your spot."
What can I say?
Sorry, Coach, but I can't play
because I'm pregnant?
Forget it.
So I just shrug and leave Coach
shaking his head.
And when Sethany finds out,
she stares me down
like I stabbed her in the back.
But I've got no choice.
I can't tell them why.
I can't even
tell myself.

Too Tender

They ache.
This morning
strapping on my bra
causes way too many
decibels of pain.
If anyone so much as
bumps into me,
they'd better plan
their eulogy.

Daydream

Any day now
my period will start.
Any day now
menstrual cramps will crush
the kernels of fear
quickly greening in me
like saplings.
Any day now
I'll be plain old fifteen again,
a girl passing silly notes in class,
giggling at the sight
of condoms.

Wish-less

Cake or no cake,
I knew I was too old
for wishing.

36B

I study myself in the shower,
unable to deny
my breasts are bigger,
just like they show you
in those sex-ed movies.
I hold them up,
figure they must be
a 36B now.
It's almost funny.
I used to wish for this.

Nobody Told Me, and If They Did, I Forgot

Why do I even bother
leaving the bathroom?
Leaving home?
I might as well
hang a sign around my neck:
Warning: Steer clear.
Girl about to barf.

Silent Lie

I hope Mom doesn't make a habit
of coming home early.
"I know the regular season's over,
but doesn't your volleyball club
practice today?" she asks.
Here's where lying
would come in handy.
I try another tack,
pretend not to hear her,
then hurry to my room,
calling over my shoulder,
"Homework!"

Punishment

What else would you call it?
I know girls
who have sex every day
and walk away.
Me, I break God's law once,
and look what it gets me.
If this isn't punishment,
I'm missing the point.
But then I think of Mary,
who God gave a baby
just because he wanted to,
and she didn't do anything wrong.
So maybe punishment
is not the point
after all.
I don't know, Lord.
I don't know anything, right now.
Color me confused,
and scared.

Ad

I feel like
one of those ladies
in the commercial
about allergies.
She's walking around in a fog,
and everything is fuzzy,
especially around the edges,
and no matter
how many times she blinks,
nothing seems clear.
That's how it is for me.
I don't want anybody
to notice, though.
So I try to smile
when I catch anyone
looking at me,
and I keep going
through the motions.

Mirror

I used to love
the full-length mirror
on my bedroom door.
Not anymore.

Sleepless

I wake in the middle of the night,
fingers fluttering over my rising belly.
My mind is split between
worry and wonder.
This inchworm of a life
taking root in me
is suddenly real.
How did I get here?
How could I be so stupid?
What am I going to do now?
I reach for *Mary, Mary,*
searching for answers,
but the words all blur.
How many tears are left in me
is anybody's guess.
All I know is,
I had enough to last me
through the night.

Bedtime

Home again,
I hurry to my chamber.
My cloak barely hides
the changing contour
of my belly.
Soon enough I will look
as though I swallowed the moon.
I must tell Joseph
that the life nesting in me
was placed there by Jehovah.
But why would he believe?
What if, convinced I have broken
God's holy law,
he drags me before the priest,
has me judged and sentenced
to be stoned?
What if—
The bloodied face of Salome
floats to the surface of my mind.
Stop it! Stop it!
I order myself.
Where is your faith?
Do you truly believe
God Almighty would bless you
to carry his son,
then stand idly by
while both your lives are taken?
I bow my head,
soak in the silence,
and wait for my heart to slow.
Lord, forgive me.
I know you will protect us.
Please ready me for
whatever trials lie ahead.

Good News

Wringing my hands,
I wait by the well
at the foot of the last *tel*
Joseph must climb
on his way home.
He is pleased,
though surprised,
to see me.
We trade holy kisses
and mount the hill in silence.
Joseph is the first to speak.
"What brings you out
to meet me?"
"Well, I — I, uhm —"
"Yes?"
I look around,
then lead the way
to a grove of olive trees
where we can be alone.
"Mary," says Joseph,
"why are you being
so mysterious?"
"Joseph," I whisper,
"do you believe in
the mysterious?"
Before he can answer,
I squeeze out the truth.
Once the words
are in the air,
Joseph stares at me, silent.
The weight of the pain
and doubt in his eyes

presses me to the ground
and holds me there
till I feel faint
and finished.

Aftermath

At long last,
Joseph finds his voice.
I tremble at the sound of it.
In pinched tones, he says,
"I care for you, Mary,
and will not turn you over
to the priest.
But come tomorrow,
I will give you papers
of divorcement.
You will then be free to go
wherever you wish,
only please,
go from here."
A tear on his cheek,
Joseph turns his back on me
and heads for my father's house,
our hearts blending
with the darkness.

Wrath

God, you must be
mad as hell.
I made you a promise
and stomped on it.
Go ahead.
Tell me you're angry.
I know I'd be.
Can't stand to look at me?
That makes two of us.

Lonely Night

My bed and pillow both
seem made of rocks.
There is no sleep to be found.
Even my thoughts toss and turn.
If I were still a little girl,
I could curl up next to Mother,
let her tell me
everything will be alright.
Lord Jehovah,
please be my mother
tonight.

Fat

Who will want me?
No more tight abs to show off
at the beach.
No slender waist to catch
a cute boy's eye.
Four months and look at me!
Soon, I won't be able to see
my feet anymore.
Or, I could be lucky
and stay pretty small, like all
the women in our family.
Yeah. Like I've been lucky so far.
Look at me! I'm hideous!
There's not much to do about it
except cover all the mirrors
in my room,
and race past
all the rest.

Comfort

I crawl into bed,
pull Mary's words to my chin
like a warm blanket.

Her faith is so strong.
Maybe if I keep close
it just might rub off.

Morning Has Broken

I.
I rise
like any other morning,
inviting Jehovah
into my day.
"Shalom, Father," I whisper.
Whatever waits for me
is at Jehovah's choosing,
and I chose, long ago,
to put my trust in Him.

II.
Joseph arrives at my door
before breakfast,
no parchment of divorce
in either hand.
"Mary," he says,
eyes gleaming with new light,
"in the dead of night,
in the deepest heart of sleep,
an angel came
and told me
all the words you spoke
were true.
He said that
I should marry you
as planned."
The sun and I stand still.
"And?"
I wait, and wait,
and wait until
Joseph, my Joseph,
sings out,
"I will!"

If Only

Alone on the rooftop,
I mourn the sunset.
I am in no great haste
to keep the promise
I made myself at sunrise:
to tell my parents.
If only Joseph's angel
would speak to them first!
Joseph kindly offered
to stand with me.
Yet, I declined. This
I must do on my own.
But what words can I use
to convince my parents that
everything will be alright?
Raised in God's shadow,
nursed on the Mosaic Law,
I have been a regular at Temple
all my life,
have daily listened to
my mother humming psalms
as she grinds meal for flatbread.
I have priests for kinsmen,
and am daughter to
a righteous man.
So how, Lord,
am I to tell my parents
that their unmarried daughter
is with child?
And once my words shatter
their dreams for me,
will they ever be able

to look me in the eye again?
I breathe deep,
descend the stairs,
and pull Gabriel's words round me
like a cloak.
One look at my face
and my mother draws near.
"Mary? What is it, child?"
My tears come quickly.
"Oh, Mother!"

Fear

Ask me what I fear most:
my mother's eyes
welling with disappointment,
wondering where
she'd gone wrong.

Their Eyes

They watch me now.
They do not mean for me to notice,
but I do.
I wish I had some remedy
for their disbelief
and disappointment.
I cannot decide
which hurts worse.

Watching

These days,
I feel Mom's eyes on me
every time I leave a room.
Some mornings,
she's Lois Lane
grilling me over Frosted Flakes:
"I haven't seen that shirt before."
"Is that the new style,
shirt hanging out your pants?"
"Don't girls wear belts anymore?"
"Honey, are you gaining a little weight?"
Sometimes, she's Superman,
still as stone,
mum as Clark Kent,
but looking for all the world
like she's got
X-ray vision.
That's when I know
I can't keep the truth from her
forever.

Warm-Up

Lately,
every day after school
I speed-walk round the track
once or twice,
doing my best to dodge
all the boys warming up
for baseball practice.
So what if I can't play
my own sport right now?
I refuse to grow
gross and flabby
just because.
Eyes straight ahead,
I charge past
a clump of kids
and leave them
eating my dust.

Slickwillow@znet.com

"i'm pregnant," I write.
"i guessed," answered Sethany.
"there had 2 be some reason
ur sick all the time.
other kids notice 2 btw.
i was just waiting
4 u 2 tell me,
on ur own."
"yeah. well, i don't know
how i'm gonna tell my mom."
"what did trey say?"
"didn't tell him yet, either."
"what r u waiting 4?"
I'm not sure
how to answer that.
Eventually, I type in
"armageddon."

Friend

"Shalom!"
A voice melodious as a lyre
fills the family courtyard.
There is only one person it could be.
I throw my arms around Hadassah,
my girlhood friend.
As ever, I am happy when
she comes to visit me.
She greets my parents before
we climb to the roof
for a leisurely hour
of weaving and conversation.
After trading ordinary news,
we work side by side,
silent at our hand looms
while the sun lavishes her warmth
on our spring afternoon.
Too soon, though,
the silence grows heavier than
I am used to.
Hadassah is the first
to shatter the stillness.
"You have changed
since I saw you last," she says,
noticing that I am larger
than she remembers,
though not knowing why.
Thankfully, the billowing
folds of my garment
do much to hide my belly
four months swollen with child.
I wave off Hadassah's comment,

as if there were
no truth to it,
and weave on,
wondering if she will
press the point.
Thankfully, she does not.
Yet, I can almost feel her
penetrating stare,
hungry for the one secret
I can never share.
But suddenly I realize
the perfect way
to throw her off the scent.
"Have I mentioned
that Joseph and I
are soon to wed?"
Hadassah's hands leave the loom
long enough to clap for joy.
"I knew it!" she cries.
"Tell me everything."

Gone Shoppin'

I try on shirts
with Sethany for company.
She stares at me,
stares at my reflection
in the mirror,
eyes lingering on
my lower half.
She makes faces
at my belly
till I have to laugh.
Of course, we both know
there's nothing funny
about my trouble.
"Time to tell Trey," says Sethany,
catching me off guard.
I cut my eyes at her.
"Hey! That's all I got to say
on the subject."
Which means
she's just getting started.
"Seth!"
I groan loud enough
for her to hear.
"It's gonna be rough,
still, the daddy
needs to know."
On and on she goes.
"I'm not saying
it's gonna be easy,
but at least you know
God'll give you the words."
I snort. "Yeah. If he's still

talking to me."
"Ooooh," says Sethany.
"I see. So, you're telling me
God forgives murderers,
but can't forgive you.
Well, that's a new one."
Sarcasm aside, she's got a point.
"Say you're right,"
I concede,
"so what?"
"Get up in his face
and spit it out," says Sethany.
"Don't go shy all of a sudden."
I nod, whisper, "Okay."
Then Sethany switches her attention
to new shirts I should
try on.
"Look at this one," she says,
holding up a green number.
"It'll bring out your eyes."
Then, she surprises me
with a hug,
guessing how badly
I need one.

Soft

Soft as fleece,
God's forgiveness
falls over me
like a quilt,
and this time,
I let it smother
my guilt.

Mister: FYI

The next morning,
I feel strong enough
to carry out my plan.
Today, I'll tell Trey, I think.
Him first, then Mom.
That settled,
I march into school
and wait by Trey's locker.
I lean against the door,
close my eyes,
and let the combination lock
dig into my spine —
anything to keep me
from feeling numb.
"I got some treasure in there
I don't know about?" asks Trey.
I look up, part my lips
and manage, "Hi."
"Whoa! This mean
you talking to me again?"
Tell him. Go on!
"Trey, I — uhm, I — "
My mouth fails,
my practiced speech
becomes a heap
of dead syllables
crushed between my teeth.
"Cat got your tongue?" says Trey.
I nod, turn away,
but somehow stop myself
from running.
Do it. Do it!

I tell myself,
then turn back,
wrap my tongue
around the truth,
and throw it like a ball,
hard as I can
till it hits home.
"Trey, I'm pregnant.
And it's yours."

Ricochet

"I'm too young
to have a kid,
and so, I don't,"
says Trey.
"You need to take
that fairy tale
to some other fool."
His words ricochet
inside my head,
hot and deadly.
"There is no one but you,"
I say.
"Oh, yeah? And how do
I know that's true?
Because you say it?"
Trey slams his locker door
like the period
at the end of his sentence,
and he's gone.
The bell rings,
and I'm left gasping
in the hall.
Glad there was a wall
to lean on.

Fog

Blinded by fear
masquerading as teardrops,
I feel my way
to the school exit,
and leave, lost,
struggling to register
a new definition
of lonely:
the baby growing inside of me
the only company
I can count on.
And, maybe, if I'm lucky,
God.

Odd, that I hardly
feel my feet
as I wander the streets
pointed toward Broadway.
I turn, on automatic pilot,
pass the Audubon Ballroom
and the ghost of Malcolm X,
wishing, if only for a moment—
Lord, forgive me—
wishing I could join him,
that I could simply
disappear.

Movies & Popcorn

It's Friday night.
Mom sticks her head in the door,
waving a video cassette.
I bet it's some old-school flick
like *Casablanca*.
She loves that stuff.
Not me, but I love her.
Plus, its our ritual,
huddling on the sofa
close as bone and skin,
in celebration mode,
ticking off another week gone by
and us alive and well
despite the dangers of these streets,
this world.
Just us girls.
But I can't risk cuddling anymore.
So when Mom says, "Come here, baby"
and reaches out,
I shout, "Stop calling me baby!"
before I'm sure my mouth
is even working.
Mom leaps back from the punch.
Softer, I say, "I'm sorry. It's just that
I'm not a baby anymore."
"Well," Mom says,
"I guess you've grown up, overnight."
She sighs. "Alright. I stand corrected."
I nod, wanting to hug her,
wanting to squeeze away the heap of hurt
that makes her shoulders slump,
but if I get too close,

she'll feel the bump and know.
So I sit at one end of the sofa,
and Mom sits at the other.
For the first time
we're together,
alone.

Birthday

Mom's twenty-nine. Again.
So I count out candles for her cake,
numbering her fake age.
I light them, one by one,
wondering why her real age
is such a mystery,
wishing she had a driver's license
I could check.
Not that her age matters to me,
but I'm curious why
she sometimes gets furious
if I press the point.
Is there some scary story
threaded through the truth,
or have I just been
watching too many movies?

The Last Supper

Last Communion Sunday
marked me as villain.
Never mind that I sat in the pew
with yards of blue cotton-polly
and an oversized vest billowing
out around me.
Cool camouflage, right?
But hardly good enough
for God.
"Prepare your hearts for the feast,"
said Pastor Grant.
"All are welcome at the Lord's Table."
I sat up straight to wait
for the holy tray.
I've always loved Communion.
"But take heed," Pastor warned.
"Do not eat the bread, or drink the cup
unworthily.
For some, doing so,
have died."
I fell back against the pew
as my secret sin gave me two
swift kicks, and sent my heart racing.
Did anybody see?
Mom sat right next to me.
I snuck a peek
but found her lost in prayer.
Eyes closed, she sent the tray my way.
The silver rim all but singed my fingertips.
I quickly passed it on
without taking my share,
too scared to even dare
a look.

Devotions

At long last,
I crack my Bible open,
finger the fragile pages
of Luke, chapter two,
and review the old story of Mary.
Jealous, I read how Joseph
stood by her
even though the kid
wasn't his.
But the Spirit whispered
Reread the passage,
so I did.
And there it was:
a reminder that God
gave Joseph
a giant push
in the right direction,
sent him a dream,
and an angel, no less.
Details.

Delirious

I look in the mirror,
but don't recognize
the girl I see.
Suddenly, she's some
scared-crazy kid
entertaining fleeting notions
of throwing herself
down a long flight of stairs,
or lingering over thoughts
of abortion.
Like I don't know
how God feels about that.
Like I could forget
for more than two seconds.
But Lord, you tell me:
What, exactly,
am I supposed to do
with a baby?

Missing You

I sit at the computer,
volleyball between my legs.
(Never thought I'd miss those drills!)
To hold the ball still,
I squeeze my thighs.
Someone told me
it's a good exercise, but who?
Anyway, Seth's latest IM
says the VB club misses me,
especially after tanking
three games in a row.
"Ouch!" Seth types,
and I reply,
"Maybe I should come back,
baby bump and all."
LOL pops up on the screen,
and I almost do.
Almost.

Options

I tell Mom I'm quitting
the volleyball club, for now,
so she can save
all the slave wages
she pays out for dues.
Of course, she asks why.
I only half lie,
telling her I'm just too tired
this season.
Tired or not, nothing stops me
from dreaming of a future.
When I graduate,
I want to be a teacher.
At least, that's what I thought
when I was ten.
Then again,
I could be a librarian.
That way, I would spend my days
swimming in a sea of books.
Before I sign on
for desk duty, though,
I'd like to make
the U.S. volleyball team,
go to the Olympics
and kick some butt.
Truth is,
I haven't settled on
a profession yet.
All I know for sure is,
when I grow up,
I (still) want to be
a girl with options.

Fama malum quo non aliud velocius ullum.

"Nothing moves faster than gossip."

— Virgil, *Aeneid,* IV, 174

Plague

I walk the school halls
behind an invisible wall,
cut off from the rest of the world.
It doesn't matter
that I carry small.
I'm Pregnant Girl,
not supergeek, not freak,
not girl-jock, or even
plain old Mister.
I'm just a girl in trouble.
Ask anyone, and they'll tell you
no other identity applies.
And if you're wise,
you'll keep your distance.

Hollywoodland

If I see one more
young and giddy
mother-to-be,
I'm slamming that remote
right down the TV's throat.

Photograph

After homework,
I hurry online,
surf my way to
my picture gallery
and scroll through
last year's photos
of me and the team.
I sure looked wicked
in my volleyball uniform.
I sure was having
a sweet time.
I sure wish I knew
if either thing
will ever be true
again.

Confession

I waited for her
on the sofa,
let winter's darkness
sweep into the room
and swallow me whole.
Home, at last, Mom
switches on the light,
notices me fighting
back tears,
and rushes to my side.
"What's wrong, baby?"
she asks,
her mom-o-meter
off the charts.
Here I am
about to break her heart,
and all she's worried about
is me.
Wordlessly, I take her hand,
place it on my belly,
and cry until
my eyes run dry.
She holds me whispering,
"It's okay, baby.
I think I already knew.
I just refused
to believe."

The Wedding

After hours of bathing,
I cover myself to keep
my swollen belly secret,
then let Hadassah anoint
my head and shoulders
with Rose of Sharon, and other
favorite sweet oils
before I dress.
Less than five minutes later,
a flicker of torchlights
brighten my window
to let me know the procession
is about to begin.
In sweep Joseph's friends, and mine
ready to spirit me away
to Joseph's house—
my home to be.
According to tradition, we
form a happy parade
dancing through
the night-drenched streets
of Nazareth
until we reach Joseph's door.
The crowd pushes us together
so the feasting can begin.
The tables are laden
with many tasty dishes,
but I have no appetite.
"Let him kiss me with the kisses
of his mouth," quotes one friend.
"Your love is sweeter than wine,"
recites another.

"Arise my love, my fair one,
and come away."
All the night long,
as wine flows,
psalms and poems,
sweet stories and love songs
swirl about us,
the strains of pipe
and lyre filling the spaces
in between.
This marriage merrymaking
is all I had ever imagined,
except for the awkward glances
between Joseph and me,
or that my right hand
would so often leave his left
to rub my belly
when no one was looking.
Then, to my surprise,
Joseph places his hand over mine,
looks deep into my eyes,
and smiles.

At Last

Two years of engagement
and preparation
are now rolled up
like a scroll.
A night of feasting
is finished, and finally
Joseph and I are led
to the nuptial chamber.
Alone, at last,
my new husband
lights the oil lamp,
then turns his back
while I free myself of my
wedding finery.
I shiver shyly, and hang my head.
None, save God and Gabriel,
have seen me thus.
It was not supposed to be like this,
my belly already swollen,
my body misshapen,
no longer the slender girl
I once was.
How can Joseph bear
to look at me?
Suddenly, all I want to do
is disappear.
"How beautiful you are,"
Joseph whispers,
wishing to ease me, no doubt.
Instead, his words
send more blood rushing
to my cheeks.

Gentle Joseph draws me
to the wedding bed,
but only to hold me.
We will not truly be man and wife
until the life inside of me sees the sun.

Sirocco

Like a wild desert wind,
some days
like this one
my feelings swirl
sudden and angry
for no reason
I can find.
Mother insists
this is normal for
a woman with child,
but I hate it.
I beat the floor
with my broom
and take my anger out
on dust and dirt,
trying to sweep my
momentary rage
out the door before
poor Joseph wanders into
the eye of the storm
that is me.

Changes

I have never been
one for tears.
Even as a little girl,
a fall or cut
might make me
bite my lip,
but nothing more.
Now, it seems
tears come easily
and often.
Just last night
I cried myself to sleep.
Joseph tried to comfort me,
but how could he understand
my desperate longing
for the old me,
the one whose belly
was flat enough
to nestle comfortably
on her side
any time she pleased?

Easy

I always thought
Mary had it easy,
her knowing all along
God was the one
who wrote her story.
Guess I was wrong.
Turns out
she needed God
as bad as me.

Her Turn

Tears spent,
Mom brings me a cool cloth
to wipe away the evidence.
Between dabs, I notice
her shoulders sagging
from something heavier
than fatigue.
Maybe I shouldn't have told her,
I think.
Look how it's weighing her down.
"This year, I'm really twenty-nine," she says.
I nod, waiting
for the punch line,
wondering what her age
has to do with anything,
wondering what's worthy
of all her hand-wringing.
"You're a smart girl," she says,
glancing up at me briefly,
then looking away.
"Once I told you my real age,
I knew you'd put two and two
together."
My math skills
are failing me now.
I have no idea
what Mom's getting at.
Then, without further ado,
she lets the truth fly.
"Mary Rudine," she whispers,
"I'm twenty-nine now,
which means
I was fourteen
when I had you."

What?

One word.
That's all I had breath for.
"What?"
After all these years
of Bible,
of "God said,"
of "wait."
After coaxing me to do
the silver ring thing
she tells me this?
Not that she sinned,
but that she was
as young as me?
What exactly am I supposed to do
with this piece of information?
So many questions
pounding my mind to mush,
but only one word
makes it to my mouth:
"What?"

Why?

"I didn't want
to give you permission
to be like me," Mom says.
"To make the same mistake.
It's a hard life, honey."
This stranger's words
build a wall between us.
I'm mad as hell
and I tell her.
Only, once I do
I realize it's not true.
What I really feel
is robbed.
She stole
the straight-shooter I knew,
left behind this double-talker
who can teach me, what?
How to lie to my kid
when the time comes?
"You know why I told you
the truth now?
So you'd know
I understand what
you're going through."
I roll my eyes
and stomp out of the room
for emphasis.
I needed you to be my rock, Mom,
is what I'm thinking,
a hefty boulder that could
bear my weight,
not some small, smooth stone
washed up on
the same shore as me.

Pretender

"Always tell the truth,"
Mother used to say to me.
Who's the liar now?

Teen Mom

One week since Mom's
big confession,
and I'm still asking
how did I miss the signs?
The way it seemed
she was in school forever,
first high school, then college,
Grandma filling in the blanks
of her absences.
There I was thinking
my mom's just going back to school
as an adult,
me patting her on the back,
proud that she did it,
proud that she looked young as
all her classmates.
Talk about stupid!
Guess the last laugh's
on me.

Need

I can't hate her now.
I need her too much,
especially since
she knows what it takes
to do this mom thing,
to have a kid
when you're a kid.
It's not like
they teach this stuff
in school.

On Second Thought

She lied to me, yeah.
But it must have been hard,
homework at the table
squeezed in between feeding me,
and running off to work
at night.
I might have noticed, except
she more than made the grade
as mom.
Hardly ever complained,
now that I think about it.
How'd she do that?
Okay, so she lied to me.
So what?
She loved me up one side
and down the other.
Nothing hypocritical
about her hugs,
now was there?

Zombie Prayer

Dead on my feet,
too many nights of no sleep,
and teachers wonder why
I nod off in class.
This forced exile
on my back
is too tough to take.
I daydream about detaching
this protrusion,
setting it on a table
at bedtime.
Jesus, I'm begging you.
Please let me sleep on my side
just one night, Lord.
Just one!
I swear,
I'd do anything you ask.
Try me.

Word's Out

I feel funny
sitting in youth group,
the half moon of my belly
putting space between me
and everybody else.
But that's okay.
I'd rather sit with Mom anyway,
feeling the cozy blanket
of her love
warming me up
in the pew.

Could be Worse

Folks at church
treat me better
than I imagined.
Sure, I get a couple of looks,
but mostly it's ladies saying,
"We're praying for you, honey,"
or "Let me know
if there's something I can do."
You'd think I grew
a few extra mothers.
Some days,
it's enough
to make me cry.
I don't think
it's their words, exactly.
I don't know.
Maybe it's God
reminding me
I'm not as alone
as I thought.

News

Last night's news
was a shocker.
A fifteen-year-old girl I know
was killed by a drunk driver.
A drunk driver!
It's not like I knew her well,
but still.
Our volleyball team
played against her's
last season.
I can see her now,
standing at the serving line,
alive as *anything*.
It's crazy.
You could be scoring points
for your team one minute,
and the next,
suddenly not *be*.
That's when it hit me:
There are worse things
than being fifteen
and pregnant.

Picture Perfect

Mom makes sure
I see the doctor
once a month.
"Are you taking your vitamins?"
"Yes."
"Any spotting?" she asks.
"No."
"Good! Let's hear that heartbeat."
It all gets to be routine,
until she suggests
a sonogram.
No biggie, I tell myself.
She spreads some jelly
on my belly,
hooks me up
to a monitor,
and—voila!
Something moves
on the screen.
Little elbows,
little hands,
little feet,
little toes,
doll-sized head,
perfect mouth,
perfect nose.
It's a baby!
A real, live baby in there!
A baby!
And it's mine.

Self Serve

Early Saturday morning,
I speedwalk to the park
bouncing the ball of my belly.
I head straight for the VB court,
then sit on the sidelines
like some old fogey,
and stare at a stranger
serving up what used to be
my game.
I raise my arms
like memory,
imagine I am helping that ball
clear the net.
I never met a volleyball
I didn't like,
only now, it doesn't like me.
That's silly, I know,
but try telling that
to my heart.

Six Months and Counting

At the Saturday matinee,
Sethany and I surrender our tickets
and make a beeline
for the popcorn concession.
With prying eyes sizing up
my supersized belly,
I'd just as soon skip it.
But Sethany says,
"What's a movie
without popcorn?"
So, I stuff my shame
and feign nonchalance better
than any Oscar-winning actress.
Thankfully, we get in a line
that moves in record time,
and we're soon enshrined
in the blessed twilight
of the theater, where
for 141 minutes,
plus previews —
I get to be
just another kid
in the dark.

Heartsound

I lay on the dressing table,
wrapped in a thin gown,
and yards of awe.
Obviously,
I'm no stranger
to basic biology,
or human anatomy.
I understand the work
of lung and aorta.
So explain to me
why the sound
of a simple heartbeat
suddenly seems more
like magic.

The Naming

From now on,
boy or girl,
my baby's name
is Junior.
After seeing her
busy little fingers,
his sturdy little thighs,
the word "it"
no longer applies.

Shadowboxing

Maybe it's
something I ate,
something I drank,
something I should have.
Whatever the reason,
Junior's got me
against the ropes,
kicking like crazy,
sparring in the dark.

Quiet

My days are quiet
without Mother near
to chide me
or join me round
the grindstone,
or tempt me with a spoonful
of some savory new stew
from her cooking pot.
A lover of silence,
even I have had enough.
Come quickly, little one!
Fill this home with the music
of voices.
The life of a new wife
is too lonely.

Cravings

No matter what Joseph says
there are still lentils to be found
in the marketplace,
though I have purchased
more than my share.
And who could blame me?
Is there anything better than
chopped leeks and garlic
simmering in a lentil stew?
Joseph wrinkles his nose
as he crosses our threshold,
day after day, after day.
I smile a weak apology,
wanting nothing more
than another bowl
of that delicious stew.

Whispers

I trudge to the village well
in the heat of the day,
anything to avoid
those nasty gossips.
My secret joy
is cleverly hidden beneath
two layers of clothing
falling in folds, and folds,
and folds of softest wool.
Even so, at six months,
neighbors begin
to count the full moons
since my marriage.
I hear them wonder aloud
how Joseph's seed
could so quickly
take root in me.
No one dares charge me
to my face, of course.
They simply lace their speech
with gossip about
the girl who is, perhaps,
too soon with child,
all the while
pretending piety.
God!
Please deliver me
from this vicious venom!

Beginnings

I wish they would widen
the spaces between market stalls.
All I seem to do anymore
is squeeze between small spaces.
I suppose I am just too —
Oh!
Leah and I bump bellies.
She is the first to laugh
and soon, I join her.
"Shalom, Mary," she says.
"Shalom, Leah."
She is a neighbor
I have scarce shared
ten words with before.
I suppose it is because
she is a few years older,
though that hardly matters,
now that we are both
mothers-to-be.
We have much in common.
We interrupt our shopping
to trade notes on midwives,
and whose expected one has
the strongest kick.
I love Hadassah,
but I long to have a friend
who truly understands
what I am going through.
And now, thank God,
I do!

Preparation

Three days running,
Joseph has missed
the evening meal.
I ask why,
but all I get for an answer
is "busy."
Enough!
Even a strong man
grows weak without food.
I waddle about the house
throwing together a basket
of bread and cheese,
figs and grapes,
and a skin of wine.
I make my way
to his carpentry shop
out back.
Heavy as I am,
I manage to slip in
without drawing his attention.
Yet I am the one in for
a surprise.
Joseph, brows knit
in concentration,
bends over a handcrafted
baby bed.
I gasp at its beauty,
and Joseph, startled, looks up.
"Well, now you see," he says.
"The sanding is almost done.
All that remains
is a bit of carving."

I find it impossible to speak.
"Now that you have taken a peek,
what do you think?" asks Joseph.
I lay a hand over my heart
and let the love in my eyes
say all.

a•dopt, *v.t.* **1.** to choose for or take to oneself; make one's own by selection or assent: *to adopt a name or idea.* **2.** to take as one's own child, specif. by a formal legal act.

— The American College Dictionary

Adoption

Mom mentions the *A* word
and I shiver from heart
to heel,
asking why my own mother
would advise me
to throw Junior away.
"It's not like that," she says.
"It's love giving life a chance.
It's giving the gift of joy,
girl or boy,
to an anxious couple
waiting for a child
to pour their love into
like a holy, healing potion.
So trash the notion
of throwing your baby away."
My pulse pares down
to a steady rhythm.
"Did you ever consider
giving me away?"
"Things were different then,"
says Mom.
"I never would have seen
your sweet face again.
Nowadays, with open adoptions,
that's all changed."

I nod, understanding
at least a little.
"No promises," I tell her,
giving Junior
a reassuring rub.
"I'll think about it."
At least,
I can chew on it now
seeing as how
the word *adoption*
no longer leaves
a bad taste
in my mind.

20 - 20

These days
when I pass Trey
in the hall
smooth-talking
his latest,
all I feel for him
is sorry
'cause underneath those
lovely lashes,
his eyes are dead.
Funny how
I finally
notice that now.

Waterlogged

Damn.
Sorry Lord, but
some gremlin must've
snuck into my room
in the middle of the night
and jammed syringes full of water
into my ankles. Again.
Tell me they don't look
like blowfish
attached to the anchors
of my feet!

LaVonne Taylor

LaVonne squeezes up
to the lunch table
at eight months,
her belly nearly big enough
to rest her tray on.
She's an island in a sea
of cool kids
and I can't stand to see her
all alone, again.
That will be me real soon.
I pay for my sloppy joe
and OJ, and make my way
across the cafeteria.
"Mind if I join you?" I ask LaVonne.
"You sure you want to?
Might give you a bad name," she says.
"The way I figure," I tell her,
"we're two of a kind."
LaVonne snorts,
eyeing my middle.
"Not yet.
You're hardly showing.
Just wait."
Why do the last two words
weigh heavy on the air?
I don't care to examine that question,
so I distract myself with another.
"Are you going to keep it,
or give it up for adoption?" I ask,
settling on the bench.
"Keep what?"
"The *baby*."

"You crazy?"
LaVonne explodes.
"You see the way it's already
messed up my life,
like the fact
I ain't got one?
Keep it? Hell no!
The second this thing
is outta me, it's history."
I shudder, afraid to fathom
exactly what she means.
"If you feel that way, then why—"
I catch myself
sticking my nose in.
"Never mind."
LaVonne's cheeks balloon
then, ever so slowly,
her anger fizzes out, like air.
"I waited too long," she mutters.
"So sue me."
I hunch over
my mediocre lunch,
wolf it faster than I should,
and jet at the jangle
of the change bell.
As I hurry through the halls,
I touch my stomach, thinking,
Don't worry, Junior.
It's not like that
with you and me.
Lonely, my disappointment
pricks like a needle
burning through my skin.
"It's all right,"

God whispers in my ear.
I hardly hear him, though.
I'm just glad it didn't take long
to find out how wrong I was,
thinking LaVonne and me
shared more than
a superficial similarity.

Safe Haven

Last night,
I caught a news byte
while I set the dinner table,
something about
another baby being found dead.
"A needless tragedy,"
said the news woman.
Apparently, there's this law:
If the mom was afraid
to keep her kid,
all she had to do
was to leave him
at the nearest hospital.
No questions asked.
The newswoman moved on
to the weather,
and I went back to
arranging utensils.
In between the clink
of knife, fork, and glass,
it hit me.
I maybe had heard something
about this law before.
I couldn't exactly remember when.
Besides, I wasn't paying
attention then.

Mother's Day

Banana pancakes
are Mom's favorite
Mother's Day meal,
and I don't disappoint.
I'm less messy than
when I was a kid,
but I still hold my breath until
she takes that first bite
and smiles.
She doesn't know it yet,
but I'm treating her to a movie,
after church.
When we get there,
the pews are filled with moms
all dressed to kill.
Evangelist Pauline Devereax
gives the message.
It's all about the mother
God handpicked
for his own son,
how she's the one
we should look up to.
Don't ask how many points
Sister Pauline ticked off
to prove her argument.
My human computer
only clicked Save on one:
She trusted God.
Who made her son on purpose,
who had a purpose for his life.
She trusted God
to see her child through.

"And so should you," said Sister Pauline.
And all the church said,
"Amen!"

Proclamation

This evening on Joseph's return
from the day's labor,
his face is long, his jaw
unusually firm, as though
he has news I will not wish
to hear.
"I must go to Bethlehem,"
he says.
"Our family must be registered
for the Census."
This makes no sense to me.
Yes, I understand that
the emperor's decree is law,
but leave me? *Now?*
I breathe deep,
forcing my heart to slow.
"Husband," I say,
"the child will be here any day."
Joseph sighs and wraps me
in his arms.
"Forgive me, Mary," he whispers.
"But I have no choice."
I purse my lips and nod, thinking,
Then neither do I.
I nod, preparing
to bid my midwife farewell.
I nod, planning
what I will pack
for the journey.
"It is settled, then,"
I tell Joseph.
"We will both leave
in the morning."

Journey

What was I thinking?
The long, dry road to Bethlehem
is littered with rough rock
and regret.
Mother, I miss you!
Maybe Joseph was right.
Maybe I should have clung
to the comfort of home,
or else remained behind
with my parents until
Joseph's return.
What kept me from it?
Only that this baby feels
ready to come into the world,
and when he does,
I want both his fathers near.
And what is there to fear,
midwife or no?
Women have born children
since time began, yes?
Besides, I will not be alone.
The Lord of Heaven is at my side.
The donkey ride is slow and bumpy,
but eventually, we are there.
"Look!" says Joseph, excited.
"The foothills of Shephelah!
Bethlehem is just beyond."
The baby begins kicking me fiercely,
ready to see Bethlehem
for himself.

What If

What if
I keep my baby?
Mom lays it on me straight.
"I won't lie to you," she says.
"I'm here to help you,
no matter what.
But you need to understand
your life will be harder
than you can imagine."
I try to. I do.
What would it be like,
daily diaper duty
and me still in school?
Would I nestle Junior
in a sling
across my chest?
Slot hot bottles of formula
in my backpack between
history books
and my English journal?
Get serious, I tell myself.
High school has no
show and tell,
and Junior isn't It.
Idiot.
I curse myself
for thinking crazy.
"I'll have to get a babysitter,"
I think aloud.
"Yes," says Mom.
"And they're expensive."
And so are diapers,

bottles, vitamins, and
what about home?
My room's already
an obstacle course
of daybed, desk, and dresser.
What am I going to do,
stick her in the top drawer,
laid out on a soft bundle
of clean socks and T-shirts?
Look at this place!
Lord knows,
there's no space here
for a crib.
Besides,
my dreams for Junior
reach higher than
this ceiling.
God, I want the stars
for this kid.
At least, I want to want that,
you know?
Can you take care of him, Lord?
Take care of me?
I still want to see
whatever dreams
you always had in store
for my future.
I worry that I'm selfish,
but Mom says
I need to be true
to me,
to you.

Summer Break

Junior is especially
restless this morning.
He/she is somersaulting, I swear.
Is that possible?
"Calm down, in there," I whisper.
"Everything's okay.
School's over on Friday.
Then you'll have me
all to yourself.
And, in ten more weeks,
you'll get to see your mom.
You'll find out who she'll be.
I'll get to say hello,
and maybe say good—" *No.*
Don't go there, Mister. Not now.
"Where was I? Oh!
You'll get to play outside.
Till then, enjoy the ride."

Coney Island Blah

In a way,
it feels like any other
summer Saturday afternoon,
the usual New York swelter
chasing a gang of us kids
out to the edge of the ocean.
But this trip to Coney Island
with Seth and friends
is blah.
Sure, I can block out the stares
of nosey passengers
on the long subway ride to Brooklyn,
and there's still the flutter
in the pit of my belly
as the park rushes into view
through the train window.
But that's all the excitement
I'm gonna get for the day
'cause once I get there,
strolling the boardwalk broadway,
munching a cheesy slice of pizza
or one of Nathan's juicy hot dogs,
and digging my toes in the sand
is all I'm good for.
There's no strapping myself in
for a slow round ride
skimming the sky on
the Wonder Wheel,
or enjoying the screaming drop
of Astroland
or the Cyclone rollercoaster.
No sir.

No female whales allowed.
Maybe next summer.
If I can find a cheap
babysitter, that is.

No

"No" used to be
two squiggles on a page
that mostly meant nothing to me.
Now, suddenly,
those letters together
are like prison guards
telling me where to go,
what to do,
who to be.
Or not.
I keep asking myself
where did all my freedom go?
Then I remember:
I forgot to say no
when it counted.

Special Delivery

"My sweet boy." I coo
and cuddle him,
swaddled in white
and smelling of sweet oil,
thanks to the royal rubbing
Joseph gave him
after his birth.
Joseph was amazing,
holding my hand
through every piercing pang,
even though I squeezed his hand
till it was bloodless.
He caught the little one
as if he had done the same
a hundred times.
"Joseph the Midwife,"
I called him,
and he filled this barn
with laughter, startling
the cows and goats, I think.
I might sniff the hay and offal,
and look round this stall
meant for animals, and wonder
what it all means, that there
was no spare room for us
at the inn,
that we were forced to spend
the night in a barn.
But at this moment,
I only have eyes
for the bundle of love
who now lies
in my arms.

Jehovah-Jireh: The Lord Provides

Lord,
here is your son,
the one you shared with me.
May he grow strong
in my care, and Joseph's.
Thank you for this good man,
and this beautiful boy.
Help us, Jehovah-Jirah,
to build a sturdy frame
for his future.

August Breakfast

I'm so glad
breakfast is my friend again.
I sit at the kitchen table
dividing my attention
between bites of toasted waffle
and the beginning
of *Mary, Mary.*
Why stop at the end
when you can read it
all over again?
"I loved that book,"
says Mom,
peeking over my shoulder.
"I know. You said."
A thousand times before.
"It helped me when
I was carrying you."
Food still in my mouth
(who cares?)
I tell her,
"Me too."

Waterclock

Our trip to the Laundromat
interrupted.
The pool at my feet says
those dirty sheets
will have to wait awhile.
"Mom!"
"I'm right here, baby.
Let's get this show
on the road.
My grandchild's about
to make an appearance."
My knees buckle,
a single thought threatening
to lay me flat:
You're almost out of time.
Make up your mind
to keep your baby
or not.
I start to pant.
I can't! I can't!
I can't decide.
Not yet.

Emergency Room

I waddle into the ER,
my heartbeat
the only sound I hear.
Is this really happening?
I look around,
see the slow ballet
of nurses, doctors, and orderlies
pushing beds and wheelchairs
with patients pale as ghosts.
Are they as scared as me?
Abruptly, a rude noise breaks in,
some tinny voice
squawking from a loudspeaker,
paging Dr. so and so,
and saying STAT
but flatter than they do on TV.
Palms sweaty, knees wobbling,
I wish this were a show
I was watching.
My thoughts bounce off
the cold white walls:
I'm not ready.
I'm not ready.
I'm not ready.
I tug on Mom's sleeve.
"Mommy, let's get out of here. Please.
I don't want to be—"
OH, GOD!
What was that?
"Looks like labor,"
says a nurse.
"Come this way."

Labor 101

Not bad,
I thought at first.
A minute of crazy pain,
then several minutes to recover.
I can do this.
I can—
Oh, God!
It's okay. It's okay.
Just so long as
it doesn't get worse.

Worse

I lie in a room
with other screaming ladies,
their cries setting
my nerves on edge.
I wish they'd all go away.
Instead, there's Mom and Seth—
when did she get here?—
plus a parade of nurses
and the social worker
asking every ten seconds,
"Are you okay? Are you okay?"
No! What do you expect me to say?
I'm scared to death.
And by the way,
there's an alien in my body
bent on ripping me apart!

Eight Hours

When will it end?
I float in a river of sweat,
this baby too stubborn
to come out.
Don't know
how much more of this
I can take.
I'd keep crying, but
I just don't have
the energy.
Oh, God!
Here comes another
CONTRACTION!

Fourteen Hours

I can't take this! Why doesn't somebody
just slice me open like a melon
and get it over with?
My immune system's resistance
is nonexistent.
I'm wracked with fever,
the tail end of a cold
fanned into full infection.
A film of gunk
covers each eye,
but so what?
Right now, the only thing
I want to see
is this baby
out
of
me!

The Golden Hour

One more push
I didn't know
I had in me.
And then
that blood-soaked eel
of a human being
finally squirts out of me,
his cry
the only sound
strong enough
to drown
my pain.

Sweet

Call it amnesia,
this sweet something that
erases all traces
of birth-pang memory.
I welcome the peace
that blankets me like fleece.
Outside my room,
the social worker waits
for my decision.
I take my time,
stare into love's eyes,
and count each finger, each toe.
No math
is more beautiful.
I name him Mine,
if only for a moment.
What was it
Sister Pauline said?
Mary trusted God.
Yes.
Yes.

**Enjoy this excerpt from Nikki Grimes'
novel Dark Sons**

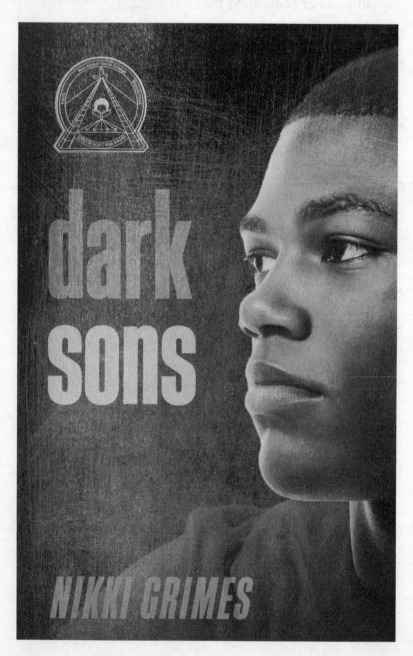

ISHMAEL

He calls himself my father.
So why is he sending me away?
This is the question
I'm tired of asking.
Better to accept what I know:
between my mother and me,
we have a bow, a loaf of bread,
a waterskin, and the clothes
on our backs.
No donkey laden with bags of grain.
No tent to pitch against the rain,
or sun, or swirling dust.
Just lonely desert ahead,
a carpet of sharp rock,
a smattering of trees,
miles of dry weed and briar,
without a settlement in sight.
We can expect a company
of wild goats or sheep,
the few sturdy inhabitants
of this terrain.
Fresh well water is bound to be
the stuff of dreams.

My head hurts from
imagining the worst.
I ignore the tears in my eyes,
pretend my father,
a few feet away,
is already dead,
and take my mother's hand.
"All will be well," I tell her,
sounding as manly
as I can muster
at seventeen,
knowing full well
that our survival
will strictly be
a matter of miracle.

SAM

The moving van
pulls away from the curb,
cutting off my air supply.
My anger a stammer,
I stare through the window
at the guy loading his car
for the move from Brooklyn to Manhattan.
He's supposed to be my dad.
I'm glad he's not waiting
for me to smile and wish him luck.
Like I give a flying—
What is he thinking,
leaving Mom in the first place?
Why does he have to run off?
To start some new family?
With *her*?
Like we aren't good enough,
like I'm not all the son
he'll ever need.
And what about tomorrow?
Child support won't put a dent
in the rent,
and Moms hasn't worked a job
in years.

I don't want to bring on her tears,

so I keep quiet, and when she

comes up to me

and slips an arm around my waist,

I say, "Yo, Mom. Not to worry.

We'll be okay. It's all good."

Sure, I know better.

This city's just waiting

to eat us up alive.

BEGINNINGS

How did I get here
at the edge of the desert,
at the edge of tomorrows
as pale as the sand?
Oh, yes!
I was born.
That's how it all began.

Dark Sons

Nikki Grimes

Betrayed, lost, and isolated, the perspectives of two teenage boys — modern-day Sam and biblical Ishmael — unite over millennia to illustrate the power of forgiveness.

A guy whose father
ripped his heart out too.
Me and you, Ishmael,
we're brothers,
two dark sons.

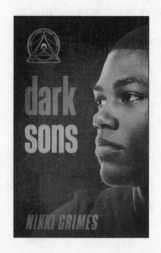

Audio and ebook editions also available.

Available in stores and online!